Laid: A Blue Collar Bad Boys Book

Blue Collar Bad Boys, Volume 5

Brill Harper

Published by Brill Harper, 2017.

This is a work of fiction. Similarities to real people, places, or events are entirely coincidental.

LAID: A BLUE COLLAR BAD BOYS BOOK

First edition. September 6, 2017.

Copyright © 2017 Brill Harper.

ISBN: 979-8223615613

Written by Brill Harper.

About this Book

Laid

Conner

I'm in over my head with these kids, but I'm all the family they have left after my sister and her husband were killed. I'm a bricklayer, what do I know about twin baby girls? Nothing. Thank God for the sweet girl-next-door.

But she's a blessing and a curse.

I've practically moved the poor girl in to help me care for these babies, but playing house is stirring up all kinds of feelings that should never see the light of day. I know she's got a crush on me, but what I want to do to her body would crush her innocence forever.

She's too sweet, too innocent, and way too young for a perv like me.

Cassidy

Mr. Webster is trying so hard to do the right thing and take care of everyone. But who takes care of him? I know under normal circumstances I would hardly even register on his radar, but lately, when he looks at me, I feel like there's more between us than there should be. Maybe more than he wants.

He works so hard. Provides for his nieces. Makes sure I'm a happy babysitter. But he's so tense. So unhappy.

I want to give him something.

Something he wants. Something he needs. Something no man has ever had before.

Me.

Author's Confession: Writing this series is like eating candy for dinner. I'm like...sorry, not sorry. Conner is the book boyfriend you

want in your life. I promise. And if you ever had a crush on the DILF while babysitting, this book is for you.

Chapter One

Conner

If someone told me a year ago that I'd be excited to find out that Magic Erasers really are magic and that one of my best friends was going to be named Roomba, I'd have throat punched him and had another beer.

I have to admit the living room looks bad. Toys strewn everywhere, blankets spread across the floor, and chair cushions in place of baby gates. I did everything in my power to stop the girls from tearing down the fucking walls, but my efforts were laid to waste by the twin tornados I call my nieces. Even now I have almost no idea where the toddlers are. I'm too busy cleaning up the mess they left behind.

I don't want the babysitter to see this mess when she gets here.

Fuck if that doesn't sound stupid. Like cleaning a house before the maid comes.

Oh man, if I could hire a maid, my life would be so much easier.

Instead, I'm running around trying to make the house presentable for the nanny so she doesn't think I'm some kind of useless loser that can't handle a few hours alone with two kids.

I just wanted to give her one night off. She's eighteen years old. She should be out with friends, dating, shopping. Hell, whatever eighteen-year-olds do. It's been too long for me to even remember.

But instead of having a carefree life, Cassidy is stuck here with me most nights. Taking care of tornado clean-up. Playing house to two babies who aren't hers and a grumpy old fucker who doesn't know what the hell he's doing unless it's the eight hours he spends outside of this house doing brickwork.

I don't know how I got so old in such a short amount of time. I'm twenty-eight, but I feel like the best of my life has passed me by already. Maybe it will get better. Maybe when I've had more time with the grief of losing my sister and her husband. Maybe when the twins can use actual words to tell me what they want and what the fuck is wrong so I'm not just trying to guess all the time.

Until then, I need Cassidy. She's an angel. The girl-next-door who stepped in the night of the accident to make sure I didn't fall down. She'd already spent the first three months of the twins' life helping my sister take care of the house and the girls after her rough delivery. Cassidy babysat or helped out whenever my sister needed, so my nieces know and trust her. Hell, they know her better than they know me. Cassidy has been with them since day one.

And now she's practically their mom.

She's somehow also managing to go to college. Her classes are online, but I don't know how she does it. So, I gave her one fucking night off, and the place is falling apart.

After wiping up sweet potato puree from the hardwood floor, I make my way toward the alarming sounds I hear coming from the bathroom. The bathroom that supposedly has a child lock on the doorknob so babies can't get into it. When I reach the open doorway, I turn on the light and freeze.

The baby in yellow, Ashley, has circumvented another child lock, lifted the toilet seat, and pushed her pretty sandals (the ones she screamed to have at Target) inside, along with her stuffed bunny. Her twin sister Hayden has shoved her tiny red dress down to her ankles and managed to pee all over it. I don't know where her diaper has gone. I don't want to know.

I don't care about the dress. I don't even care about the sandals. But I'm torn apart by Mr. Bunny.

No way Ashley will go down tonight without Mr. Bunny. She'll be up all night screaming. My life has effectively taken a turn for the worse.

I feel like I need seven more hands. I don't know where to start. How to start. I just want a goddamned beer and to watch a game on TV. But not tonight.

I start with Hayden. I clean her up, put her red pajamas on her and stick the one-year-old in her crib. Her cries are loud, but Ashley's are louder. Shrill wails paused only by incoherent mumbles that sound a lot like backtalk. Ashley is the fighter of the two, the one that causes the most trouble.

The one more like me.

After putting Ashley's yellow jammies on, I plop her in the neighboring crib, sighing as the girl screams her little lungs out. I try everything from singing, to rocking her, to kissing her angry, red cheeks. Nothing helps.

Hayden has drifted off to sleep, but Ashley is still fighting it by the time Cassidy comes through the nursery door. I guess I was so caught up in trying to soothe the baby that I didn't hear the front door open or close. Some protector I am.

Cassidy comes all the way into the room, hovering behind me. After watching me struggle, she reaches around me and picks up the crying child, hushing her.

"I was trying to calm her down, but she just wouldn't stop," I apologize, feeling like a fool. "I don't know the nursery rhymes, but she seemed to like Luke Bryan for about five minutes." Cassidy chuckles and waves me off wordlessly, motioning for me to leave the room. But I stay for a minute, watching.

She begins humming something my sister used to sing, a soft lullaby that soothes the baby in a way I can't. I really don't think I'd have been able to keep this family together without Cassidy. I'll never be able to repay her for the sacrifices she makes for my nieces. For me.

Cassidy is a slim girl, though you wouldn't be able to tell from the oversized sweatshirt she wears all the time. The glimpse I catch of her figure as she bends over the crib has me rock hard, though. The tight-fitting jeggings she wears stick to her generous thighs because she's slim but round and thick at the bottom. Lush.

I start to sweat.

It's been a long time since I've been with a woman. And it's going to be a lot longer as far as I can tell. But this babysitter shouldn't suffer the consequences of my overactive desires. It's not her fault. She's done nothing but help me, and I repay her by thinking about how I'd like to see that thick ass jiggle while I'm coming at her from behind.

She is driving me crazy.

Sometimes, her gaze lingers a little too long on me. Then she blushes and looks away. She's shy, sweet. Part of me wonders if she's biddable and pliant, too. The part of me that's an asshole.

I can't take advantage of a young woman's innocent crush. I would crush that innocence. That's not who I am. Or at least, that's not who I want to be.

But I can think about it all I want to. And I do.

When I get into bed every night, I dream she is there with me. My dreams are always about pleasuring her, making her see how beautiful she is, appreciating her body the right way. My pleasure comes from seeing her fall apart at the touch of my fingers. Hearing that sultry voice cracking as I bury my tongue deep in her pussy. Watching her breasts bounce as she comes hard around my cock.

I have to jerk off at least twice a day at this point. It's shameful, to be honest. I try to rid myself of the fantasies, but they are still there. Her innocent eyes staring up at me as I pound into her, the sounds she would make. Cassidy has taken over my mind, and there isn't much I can do to stop it. Not that I really want to.

No, what I want to do is take her. Make her mine.

By the time Cassidy comes downstairs, I am barely restraining myself from pinning her to the kitchen counter and tearing off her pants. I just can't risk coming on to her. The girls need her. I need her.

I can't lose her. She's the only thing holding my world together right now.

"She asleep?" I ask, turning in a way to hide my erection.

She nods. "Mr. Webster?" Cassidy asks. "What are you planning to do for your birthday?"

"I told you to call me Conner, Cassidy," I correct her. For her own self-preservation, she needs to use my first name. When she calls me Mr. Webster, it feels even dirtier. Taboo. Mr. Webster and the babysitter kind of thing. It shouldn't turn me on so much. The taboo of it. Christ. She's barely legal. I am such an asshole. "And I don't want to do anything for my birthday."

Birthdays are hardly anything to celebrate anymore. Just another year closer to death, basically. God, is that really me? I'm not old enough to feel this old.

She bites her lip like she's worried about what she's about to say. "I think we should do something."

"We?"

I know exactly what I want to do. And she's standing in front of me.

What I want is the right to touch her when I want to, instead of having to clench my fists. I want the right to taste her, instead of having to bite my tongue. I want her body, but I know I can't have it. I'm so frustrated. By this life I didn't ask for. By the pain those girls upstairs are going through. And by the desire for this innocent babysitter than I can never, ever act on.

"We should do something together. The girls need to be part of a normal family celebration."

"*We* aren't a normal family, Cassidy. We aren't really a family at all."

She shrinks back, and I feel like a douche.

She looks at the floor now. "You're right. I have some reading I need to do tonight. I guess I should get to it."

"Cassidy, I'm sorry."

I hate that I hurt her feelings. I know she's got everyone's best interests at heart. But I'm afraid of what will happen if we act like we're playing house any more than we already do. I don't know that I'll be able to know the difference.

She gives me a shaky smile. One I know is fake. "It's fine. I'm going to crash in my room here tonight. It's late."

She's been doing that most of the time. I don't remember the last night she went home next door. It's easier on us both, since I go to work so early. I can't imagine her parents are okay with it, but they haven't said anything. She stays in the guest room. I sleep in my sister's old room. It's all on the up-and-up. Except for the part where I want to wake her up by eating her pussy until she's screaming my name.

Chapter Two

Cassidy

I'm worried about Mr. Webster. Conner. I need to call him Conner.

He's only twenty-eight with twin girls suddenly thrust on him. I know he used to have friends, used to go out. His sister Sandy used to worry that he'd never settle down. Now look at him.

She said he had a different girlfriend every weekend. Once, after wine on the patio, our favorite evening ritual when her husband had to work late, Sandy called Conner a manwhore and we nearly peed ourselves laughing.

She loved her brother a lot. She'd be very proud of how he stepped up to the responsibility of the girls.

He tries so hard. He watches me very closely with the babies, and then he mimics what I do—to varying degrees of success. It hasn't been easy, but he put his life on hold, and he spends every bit of his energy providing for those girls.

If I weren't around, who would celebrate his birthday with him? Even if it isn't my responsibility to make him feel good, I feel like it is somehow.

My mom is worried about me, though. She thinks he's taking advantage of me. I don't have the heart to tell her, "I wish." He's sex on legs, if you ask me. Not that I have any experience with that—with Mr. Webster or anyone. Some heavy petting is as far as I've gone. I don't even know why. I'm not religious—I'm not saving myself for marriage. I just haven't been that attracted to anyone.

Before now.

I'm just too serious, I guess. That's always been my problem. I don't understand kids my own age—never have. I've always spent time with adults when possible. When Sandy and her husband moved in next door to my family, I became very close to her. She was older, but she didn't treat me like a dumb teenager. She was my best friend. I miss her every day.

When she got pregnant with the twins, I was there every step of the pregnancy. Once, when I was holding her hair as she puked, she told me she wished I was her sister. That if her brother ever settled down, she wished it would be with someone like me. Or maybe it could be me.

Like I could tame a manwhore? Right.

I laughed it off at the time. But when he came to the house the night of the accident and just stepped in despite his grief and confusion, I have to tell you, that's when it started for me. My fantasies.

He does what a real man does. He takes care of things that need to be taken care of. He puts his family before his own happiness. He works hard and never complains. He even cares that the hired help, me, doesn't get burned out.

But who takes care of him?

Men that look like Mr. Webster...Conner...don't go for serious, boring girls like me. They date party girls and models. Maybe strippers or something. I don't know. Just not girls like me. Wallflowers whose biggest rebellion was drinking wine at the neighbor's house.

I toss and turn, but it's no use. If I don't get some sleep soon, tomorrow is going to suck, big time. I reach over to drink some water and realize I forgot to refill my bottle. Duh.

I'm down the stairs and halfway into the living room when I realize the TV is on. That's weird. Usually Mr. Webster...Conner...watches TV in his room.

The first thing that appears on screen is a large crowd of men surrounding a bed, waiting their turn around one hapless naked woman. I stop walking, frozen like a statue.

Porn on the big screen looks a lot different than it does on my laptop. It's sort of mesmerizing. Lifelike.

The men start to rub their cocks all over her, touching her breasts and her face. One man slaps his cock against her cheek hard, but she just opens her mouth submissively. He immediately stuffs his length down her throat. As he does, another man is prepping her. After gauging her reaction, he wastes no time in pushing into her, bottoming out.

I've seen porn before, but I guess I'm just shocked stupid. Is she enjoying it? Is she turned on or is she zoned out and thinking about her bills or traffic or what to have for dinner?

See? This is what is wrong with me. Instead of just getting turned on by people having sex, I'm wondering if the actress is thinking about her bills.

With her head tilted back in submission and her pussy being pounded from the other end, the woman is lying limp, simply taking it. Is that enjoyable? The other men rub their dicks on her, smearing pre-cum all over her torso and thighs. She doesn't react, even when the man forces her to choke on his cock.

That's when I hear Mr. Webster...Conner...groan. And that's when I realize that slapping sound is not just the movie. He's masturbating.

I'm frozen. I can't see anything but the back of his head. But if he realizes I'm here...oh my God. My awkward life is so awkward. What do I do?

Heart dropping to the cold, wooden floor, I stand there, steeling myself. If I walk backwards very slowly, maybe he won't hear me. He's obviously very busy.

"Cassidy!" he says my name on a growl.

Shit. Busted. Instinctively, stupidly, I say, "What?"

Time stops and I wish for the earth to swallow me whole. A small part of my brain registers that he was growling my name while *masturbating*. That he didn't actually know I was standing behind him.

That I could have maybe gotten out of this without wanting to die if I hadn't responded.

Things happen fast. He jumps up, whirling toward me with his dick in his hand. He's saying things, but I don't know what they are because I'm mesmerized by his cock. It's an angry purple and big. So big. It looks hefty, like a weapon. The substantial shaft is thick and veined, and I can't tear my eyes from it. I've never seen a cock before in person. And it's still in his hand and whatever he's saying is scored to the soundtrack of the porn still playing on the big screen behind him. The moans and bodies slapping. The bad music. One guy says, "Take it, you little cock slut. Take all the cocks."

"I'm sorry!" I yell, still staring at his cock. It's huge. And I'm saying that while porn stars behind him on a seventy-two-inch screen are wanking their huge cocks. Mr. Webster...Conner...is porn star big. "Oh my God."

I don't know what else to do. So, I run. Back up the stairs. Back into my room, closing the door gently because I cannot deal with waking up the kids right now. I pace for a minute. Then I sit. Then I pace.

Everything is changed now.

Mr. Webster is not just the handsome man I work for. He's not just the beloved brother of my best friend. He's not just the neighbor who needs help.

He's sex personified. I will never see another cock again without remembering his. I sort of thought my first look at a man's penis would be during a tender moment. A sweet, treasured memory.

Instead, my first showing makes me feel unsettled by the brutal, primal feelings stirring inside me. Like something in me wants to be dominated. Used. Taken.

I shake my head. This is crazy talk. I saw his dick. Okay. So what? Move on, brain. The next time I see a man's cock, it will be inside a tender, loving relationship moment and this weird feeling will be gone and I won't even remember this night.

Right.

I move to the window and push the lace aside. I can see my bedroom at home from here. The window is dark, of course, since I'm over here. But I can't help wishing I'd made a different choice. That I was there instead of here. Awaiting doom.

This is bad. How do I face him tomorrow morning? Does he think I was pulling some stalker-like move? Ninja-watching him watch porn? Or maybe he feels bad. Like he's corrupting me. It's not his fault. It's his house, after all. He has so little privacy. I shouldn't even be here.

Except he *does* have the privacy of his own room, and I'm only here because he needs me to be.

He's got other needs, too, it would seem.

So why was he jacking off to porn in the living room instead of his own room?

And why did he say my name?

I'm almost done flushing hot and cold when he knocks on my door.

I seriously cannot do this right now. "Um. It's not a good time," I answer.

There's a heavy pause. "We need to talk. About what just happened."

"No, no, we don't. Everything is fine." Does my voice sound weird? I think I sound too chipper. It's definitely too chipper. I sit on the edge of my bed, my back rigid like I have a steel pipe for a spine.

"Cassidy, I'm coming in."

I pull my pillow into my lap, covering what isn't really very risqué sleeping clothes, but I feel exposed. Which makes no sense. I wasn't the one with my dick out.

"I apologize," he says. He's only wearing sleep pants, and they're tented up pretty far since I interrupted him before he could finish, and apparently, getting caught did not diffuse his situation. It does not look comfortable.

I need to move my eyes away from the mesmerizing snake in his pants, so I bring my gaze up. It crawls up his torso slowly. Too slowly, honestly. But his abs lead up to a rock-hard, wide chest covered with a tribal dragon tattoo.

"Cassidy," he interrupts my thoughts of my tongue tracing the dragon and I am pretty sure my face is on fire.

Oh my God, this is so inappropriate. Then I laugh. Because this is ridiculous, and I am ridiculous for worrying about my inappropriate thoughts when he was the one watching gangbang porn and flashing his dick.

I need to pull it together. I clear my throat, try to sound mature and civilized. "You don't have anything to apologize for."

I bring my gaze to the pillow in my lap as looking him in the eye is so not an option right now. *Try to be a grown-up, Cassidy.*

"The DVD player in my room stopped working. I shouldn't have been watching that in the living room. That was bad judgment on my part. I'm sorry if that made you feel uncomfortable."

I shake my head comically fast. "No, no. No problem. It's just porn, right?" Chipper again. Way too chipper.

"I guess I just don't want you to think I'm some kind of pervert. I don't want you to be uncomfortable here."

"It's your house. You can watch porn in any room you want."

"I should probably get rid of it. I don't want the girls to stumble on it."

"Well, as they get older, you might want to keep it out of their reach. But I don't think you're the only parent with porn in the house. It's fine."

He leans against my door and *thunks* his head against it. "It doesn't feel fine. I feel like I've ruined everything. I just...it's been a long time for me. I was just letting off some steam. I'm so sorry that you...well, I'm just sorry that it happened. If you don't feel comfortable..."

"No, I'm fine. Really. Everyone watches porn." *Smooth, buttercup.*

His eyebrows raise. Great. When I said "everyone" I didn't mean me. I mean, I do sometimes, I guess. But I wasn't trying to insert myself into this situation any more than I already am. Nor do I want him thinking about me watching porn. This is so wrong.

"So you don't hate me?"

"Of course not, Mr. Webster." He groans. "I mean Conner."

"Okay, good."

My God. The beast in his pants is still hard. I realize that when this conversation ends, he's going to go to his room and finish. He's going to have to. I can't stop thinking about that now. Him coming.

I don't know if size or hardness has anything to do with semen and virility. But at this moment, I'm imagining that when he comes, it's not in trace amounts. I need to stop the mental picture of him coming hard, ejaculating ropes of fluid. Erupting from that helmet-tipped cock.

"Are you okay, Cassidy? Your face just got really red."

"I'm...fine." *So not fine.*

Conner tilts his head and smirks a little at me. "Fine, huh?"

He's teasing me. I bite my lip. I have always prided myself for being mature for my age. Why am I acting so silly? I let out a deep breath. "We're being absurd, aren't we? I mean...we're two adults living in this house. It's safe to assume that since neither of us get out much, we're going to have to meet our own needs occasionally."

Conner's eyes darken. Is he imagining me meeting my own needs? Is that...does he *like* that?

This is very new territory for me. I lack experience. While I may feel more mature than others my age, sexually I'm behind. It's a strange dichotomy, feeling twenty-five and fifteen at the same time. An old soul yet naïve. Also, most girls my age don't use the word dichotomy in their internal thoughts. I don't think.

I'm hopeless.

"I know you're legally an adult, Cassidy. But in my mind, you're..."

I deflate a little on the inside. It's not Mr. Webster's...*Conner's*... fault that he doesn't understand how I've spent my whole life feeling trapped in a body too young for my tastes. That also sounds ridiculous. I know this. But nobody has ever taken me as seriously as I think they should. Not until Sandy. She didn't treat me like a kid. She saw who I am on the inside. She never patronized me.

And then after she died...I lost that support system when I needed it most. Because now I need to be the most mature I've ever been, and I'm still not taken seriously. She's gone and her kids need me. It's hard to have the weight of the world on my shoulders when most people treat me like all I care about is 1D fanfiction and the newest contouring highlighter. Everyone acts like I'm just a great babysitter. I think the only people who really understand that I'm more than that are the girls. They sensed something was wrong when their parents died, but of course they didn't understand what or why. But they did know, right away, that my role in their world had changed.

To the world, I am a teenage babysitter. But to those girls, I'm more. I thought maybe their uncle understood that, too. He says it enough, that I keep this family together. But when the chips are down, he retreats to treating me like the kid that comes over for a few hours a week and does her homework while the girls nap. Not the woman holding this house together by sheer acts of will.

"I know I'm young, but I think I've proven I'm a mature, capable person."

"Of course, you are. This house wouldn't run without you. I know that. I'm guilty of relying too much on you. But even though I see you acting more mature than me most days, you're still young. It's not an insult."

"It's not like you're over-the-hill, either."

God, his penis is still huge. "I feel like it lately. I hope I didn't shock you too badly. That movie...it was kind of hardcore."

I remember that woman and all those cocks. Of course, I blush. I can feel it. My face is burning. "It was a little, yeah. But it's okay. I'm not shocked...too much. I've watched porn before. I know it's just fantasy."

He steps into the room and sits in the desk chair. "I can't imagine you enjoying that movie, though. It was pretty raunchy."

I'm going to have to keep pretending I can handle this conversation like an adult, aren't I? He's actually talking to me like a friend, not a kid. Thirty seconds ago, that's all I wanted. Now, what I want is to giggle and pull the covers over my head.

I am such a contradiction, I don't even understand myself.

But as awkward as the topic is, I miss having someone just to talk to. Sandy and I talked all the time about everything. And it's not like I have a lot of time to talk to anyone else now that she's gone. I have some college friends, but their lives are so different from mine. And since I go to class online and spend the rest of my waking hours taking care of the girls, I don't have a lot of time to socialize.

"I, um, usually prefer to read erotica than watch porn. But sometimes..."

Next time without the "um" and you might almost pull this off.

"I'll give you some top-secret info into the secret life of men. If your boyfriend ever tries to get you to watch porn with anal, it's part of a bigger plan."

I laugh. "I don't have a boyfriend, as I'm sure you know since we practically live together."

"Yeah, I don't have a girlfriend, as you know."

Queue silence that lasts one beat too long.

"Your life has changed a lot. Sandy used to talk about you, you know. All your conquests. Maybe you're the one who needs a night out of the house."

He shakes his head. "I'm not going to lie. I miss getting laid regularly. But, the lifestyle I was living...I don't think I miss it as much as I think I do." He scrapes his hand across his stubbled chin. I wonder what that feels like. What it would feel like rasping against my skin. I forget he's talking and have to pick up the conversation in mid-sentence. "—that doesn't make sense, does it? When things are out of control here—meaning whenever the twins are awake—I wonder what happened to my life. How different it is now. But I guess, if I think about it, I don't think I could just go back to it. I just realized how empty it was."

"Am I watching you have an epiphany right now?"

He chuckles. "I guess you are." His face gets serious again. "This life is hard, but it's full." He looks up, right at me. "But you...you're too young to be locked away in this house."

"I don't feel locked away. Maybe it's because I was already here so much, before the accident. My life didn't change as much as yours did. I spent a lot of time here, with Sandy and the girls. Jake worked so much that he wasn't home as much as he wanted to be. So, I would hang out, be an extra set of hands. And be company for Sandy. I don't think I'm sacrificing as much as you think I am."

"You shouldn't be sacrificing anything at all. You're eighteen. You should be carefree and letting the boys fight over you."

"I don't...even before the accident, I didn't have boys fighting over me."

"That doesn't make any sense to me at all. You're smart and funny and kind."

"Mr. Webster," I say, using his last name very deliberately, "how many women have you fought over because they were smart and funny and kind?" His lips press into a firm line. "Guys my age find me boring. And truthfully, I'm not attracted to them, either. They're too immature."

"So, go out with older guys."

Our eyes meet. Clash really. Like he can't believe he said it. Like he didn't think about the ramifications of saying it out loud while he's still sporting a hard-on and I'm on a bed.

Say something.

"I will."

Not that.

"After things calm down here, I mean. But right now, I don't have time. For men. Um, for dating. You know what I mean. I'm busy here."

"I don't want to take advantage of you, Cassidy."

And there it is. It was couched in "the right thing to say" about me working too much as his nanny. But we both know the underlying current is more important.

"I wouldn't let you take advantage of me, Conner. I'm not naïve, at least not as naïve as you think. I can make my own decisions."

The air grows thick and a new kind of tension hums between us. An awareness.

"I should go. The beasts will be up before we know it, and we both need some sleep."

I nod. "Goodnight, Conner."

He stands, and I don't think he's any less hard than he was when he came in. He can't hide it, so he doesn't try. "Goodnight, Cassidy. Sweet dreams."

"You too."

His eyes darken and my nipples tighten beneath my T-shirt. We may have cleared the air, but I think we added more than we took away.

Chapter Three

Conner

It's been a week since the Porno Incident. While that night was awkward as fuck, I think things might actually be better now. Cassidy and I talk more. We're war buddies in the trench by day, and in the evenings, we're...friends.

I still want to fill her full of cum, don't get me wrong. But I like talking to her. I can see why she and Sandy were so close.

I rub my chest over my heart. I miss my sister so much. She'd have been the one I went to for help and advice in any other situation. But she can't help me now. Thank God she left me Cassidy.

I go downstairs and halt at the sight. Cassidy is smiling at me over her shoulder, then she returns to what she was working on at the counter, hiding whatever she's doing from my view. She's still in her pajamas, which I have to admit I like. They aren't sexy lingerie by any means. A longish T-shirt over a pair of long-john bottoms and fuzzy socks.

I like the way those bottoms show off the shape of her legs. I like knowing she's not wearing a bra. But what I love is the comfort she has in my presence now. That she doesn't feel awkward wearing her pajamas in front of me.

I kiss Hayden and Ashley on the tops of their heads. "What you doing over there, Cassidy?" I ask the girls, "Is she hiding something from me?"

They coo and Hayden offers me a Cheerio from her tray. Then Cassidy turns around. She's holding a plate with a muffin in the center of it. She's lit a single candle in it, and she starts singing a very off-key rendition of "Happy Birthday." The girls don't know the words, but they like songs, so they start banging their hands on their trays and chattering along.

I'm overwhelmed with a feeling I don't know the name of. It's warm and bright, and for the first time in six months, I am content. More than content. I feel like I am exactly where I need to be, doing exactly what I need to be doing, and a kind of peace steals over me. I can't stop the smile from splitting open my damn face.

Cassidy finishes the song and her eyes are shining with tears like she's feeling it too. Whatever it is. It's big, too big to hold inside. I want to grasp the moment, but I know it's almost gone.

"Thank you," I manage. "I can't think of a better way to start my birthday." I want to say something cheesy. I want to take her in my arms and just hold her. Hold this perfect moment before it dissolves and I feel empty again.

She holds the plate up. "Make a wish."

I don't believe in wishes. I know you either act on your desires or you don't. And the man I was on last year's birthday had very simple desires and he acted on them, fulfilling his short-term goals with ease. He didn't know what hard was. He didn't know about grief or responsibility or putting off desire because the long-term consequences outnumbered the short-term achievement.

He'd have wished for a birthday kiss from the pretty girl and then worked his way to more.

But if I did believe in wishes, right now I'd wish for this feeling, this fleeting feeling, to come around more often and stay longer. To keep the pretty girl smiling. To hear the babies chattering instead of crying. To know with bone-deep certainty that I'm the right man for this job I've been given.

So, I blow out the candle and wish that I believed in wishes.

The rest of my day goes by in a blur. We're working on a project for a museum downtown. I'm tired, hot, and grubby when I get home. I know after my shower that it's my turn to take over from Cassidy. Dinner, bath time, story time, and bed time (hopefully) with the girls so she can study and have the evening free.

When I get out of the shower, I'm surprised to find the girls already eating their dinner.

"It's your birthday," Cassidy explains. "You should relax. I'll take the evening shift."

Still, I help her with the kids. Four hands are better than two. We work well together. Ashley and Hayden are happy to have both of us at the same time. I take Ashley from Cassidy's arms when she's rocked her to sleep. It's a seamless transition now, so different from when we first started passing babies back and forth to each other. In the beginning, we used to wake them up more often than not when we tried to pass a baby to each other. Then we had to start over. Now, I can read Cassidy's body language better, and I actually know how to hold a baby. Even the tricky part of putting Ashley down in the crib without waking her is second nature.

We sneak out of the nursery, Cassidy double-checking the monitor before we close the door behind us.

"Come to the kitchen with me," she orders, and I follow her down the hall and down the stairs. Happy as hell to be behind her. God damn, her ass in those shorts is the best damn thing I have ever seen. If I keep looking, I'm going to need a cold shower, but it's my fucking birthday. If ever there's a day when I can ogle those luscious globes guilt-free, it should be today, right?

Her outfit is probably not something she thought would turn me on. The shorts aren't too small and the T-shirt is baggy. Something about the knee-high athletic socks is hot as hell, though. She looks...comfortable. At home. Relaxed. And that is the strangest thing to be turned on by, but it really works for me.

I try to think of the last woman I was with and have a hard time even remembering the guy I used to be. I used to like the girls who were all done up. Glossy lips, perfume, high heels...all of it. Now, I feel like I wouldn't even know how to act around a woman like that. Everything seemed so forced then. Not like now. I find I appreciate the shape of Cassidy even more when she's just bumming around, like tonight.

She's real.

And real sexy.

I need to pull my mind out of the gutter. She's my partner in this baby care business. I don't want to ruin the camaraderie we've established because my dick starts running the show. My dick is a horrible decision maker.

She's got a sneaky look in her eye again. I like it. "Why are we in the kitchen?"

"Cake."

"You made cake?"

She laughs. "Yeah, in my spare time, I bake. Oh wait, no, I don't. I have twins to take care of all day. Therefore, I have no spare time. I bought cake, silly."

I'm still reacting to her teasing me when she pulls a pink box from the fridge and opens it. Inside is my favorite—German chocolate. That feeling from this morning comes back, filling my chest with this light that seems to expand. Like I swallowed sunlight.

If I didn't know any better, I'd say I was really into baked goods suddenly—the muffin this morning and the cake tonight. But my sweet tooth isn't very strong. And while it's my favorite cake, even I know the feeling comes from her remembering it's my favorite flavor. From her making sure I felt special today.

Damn. She really is smart, funny, and kind. Those eighteen-year-old punks don't know what they're missing, because suddenly, those are the things that make my heart race and my palms sweat. Yeah, her ass is amazing—but her heart. Jesus. I wish I believed I deserved her heart.

I need to make this not awkward and fast. "You're not going to sing to me again, are you? Please say no."

She throws a kitchen towel at me while she pulls plates down. "Ha-ha. Maybe I should."

"Wait a minute." I put the plates back.

"Don't you want cake?" Her earnest fear that she's disappointed me is somehow like an arrow right to my heart.

"I *do* want cake. Thank you for arranging it. What I don't want is more dirty dishes. We are going to be uncivilized around here for a change." I hand her a fork and pull the small cake from the box. "Dig in."

"Just like that?" She's dubious, and I fucking love that expression on her face. She's usually so in control, especially in the kitchen. She's organized and labels leftovers and always remembers to flip the magnet on the dishwasher so we know if the load is dirty or clean. She doesn't eat cake without cutting it. Without putting in on plates.

"Just like that," I say, and take a forkful.

We're eating cake like we're getting away with something, and I realize this birthday, despite all the pain of the last six months, is the best I've had in a long time.

"We're not drinking milk out of the carton," she warns me. "Don't get any ideas."

"We might."

"No, I draw the line there."

"Live a little, Cassidy."

"Mr. Webster, you're a very bad influence on me."

And just like that, I'm rock hard.

I have very purposefully stayed away from any porn that included babysitters or barely legal teens lately. In fact, that's why I was watching the MILF gangbang last week when I got caught. I've been trying to rub out to anything that doesn't remind me of the barely legal babysitter I want to bone living in my house.

Because I sure as shit wouldn't pass her around to a group if I ever got her naked. No, I'd keep her to myself. Nobody but me would touch her, see her. Nobody but me would hear the sounds she makes when she comes. Nobody but me would know the sweet taste of her pussy.

Fuck. Now I'm really hard.

It's her fault. All week, I've been making sure not to put her in that taboo role, and then she goes and reminds me that I'm older, I'm her boss, and I am a bad influence on her. All in one sentence.

She's a very naughty babysitter.

Fuck.

"I think you might want me to be a bad influence on you, Cassidy."

She pauses her fork in mid-air, and this bubble forms around us in the heavy silence as we both think about what I just said. I hadn't meant to say it. Not out loud.

"Maybe I do."

There's no one and nothing outside of this kitchen. No chores, no responsibilities, no have-to or should-haves. The world has shrunk to this moment. To this fresh-faced girl with jade green eyes and a woman's heart but a naïve spirit. This angel who thinks she's a wallflower, but she's really a riot of roses. Not the kind you buy in the grocery store, but the heirloom kind that climb the walls and carry a rich scent that stays in your nose.

I want to tickle her skin with the soft, velvet petals. I want to fuck her on a bed of roses.

Shit. There it is.

I want to fuck her.

"Cassidy—"

"You're going to say something that makes total sense. About me being too young for you. About you being my boss. About not wanting to be involved in the cliché naughty babysitter and daddy scenario. So just save it. I get it. It's okay. I'd rather we just pretend we had the conversation, though, okay? Because I know you're right. About all of it. But it doesn't stop me from wondering what it would be like." She takes a deep breath. "And that was really hard for me to say out loud and to you. But I'm glad I did."

"I'm glad you did, too." Even in the one week since our talk in her room, she's changed. I've seen it in the little things—her teasing me more, being more comfortable around me—but her telling me flat out that she thinks about having sex with me is the biggest step I've seen her take. And it's a good one. I put the cake down. I want to start ripping clothes off her body. Knowing she wants me is a bigger turn-on than I imagined it would be. But I need to slow down. "It would be really easy to get caught up in the fantasy. Too easy. We need to think this through."

She cocks her head and looks at me through new eyes. "Thank you."

"For what?"

"For talking to me. For thinking this through with me. Instead of treating me like I don't know my own mind."

"I know you're smart. And you're mature. But that doesn't change that you are young. And I am your boss. That does make a difference. There's an imbalance of power here, and I don't want to take advantage of that." There. I sound like a full-fledged adult. I want to stab myself in the eye I hate it so much. Being an adult is overrated, and I'm sure that's why I've put off responsibility until this year.

But my words sound like I pulled them off a feminist blog. Which I did, actually. Last week when I was Googling why it was wrong to lust after my babysitter. And it is wrong. So wrong. So wrong it's right.

I'm not okay with being a dick. Taking advantage of someone important to me is not cool.

But I still want to fuck her. And if she's not being manipulated into it, is it still bad?

"Imbalance of power?"

"Yeah, okay. I read that. On a blog. Also, I'm not supposed to tell you to smile more because that's condescending. And when I sit on a train, I need to make sure I'm not manspreading."

It was a very in-depth blog, okay?

She does this squinty thing with her eyes and then shakes her head at me. "There might be a power imbalance here, but I'm not sure it's weighted on your side. Seriously, Conner, how long do you think you could run this house without me in it?"

"About an hour and a half."

She laughs. "Exactly. I could abuse *my* power. Gouge you for more money. Take more time off. Do less than I do—and you'd still put up with it because you don't have a lot of choices. I'm not here as a starry-eyed teenager you can mold." She starts to shrink into herself, but then forces her shoulders back and stands up straight. "We both know it's been me molding you into the man you want to be so you can be a father to those girls. Teaching you. Mentoring you."

My ego rears its head and wants to argue. But she's totally right. And that this little slip of a woman called me on my bullshit is fabulous. She's the kind of partner a man wants in all the ways that count.

She's sticking up for herself, and that turns me on even more than I already was.

But she's barely out of high school, and I have a feeling, based on her shyness around me, she's not had a lot of boyfriends. I'm not like whips-and-chains kind of dominant in bed, but I do have some pretty strong tendencies that would probably scare her.

But what if they didn't?

"Okay then, you have some power here. But how experienced are you?" I ask.

She blushes. "You mean sex?"

"Yeah, sweetheart. I mean sex."

She meets my eyes defiantly for about .2 seconds and then looks down. "Not very."

"That's nothing to be ashamed of. I just want you to think about what kind of changes the two of us getting closer would bring." Shit. I'm saying all the right things, but I want to give her every fucking experience there is. One after the other, over and over again.

"I'm a virgin." She starts getting busy putting the cake plate back in its box. Cleaning and organizing mode has been reengaged. I don't stop her because I know that's how she feels in control of a situation. "I know I'm not like a lot of girls my age. I'm probably too modest about my body. I'm not good at flirting." She hip checks the fridge door after putting away the cake. "And I didn't think you looked twice at me. Until...I heard you say my name. Last week. When you were..."

Yeah, that. We never talked about the fact that she heard me call her name while I was masturbating. It seemed like something better left swept under a rug.

"So, maybe we can help each other?"

My eyebrows lift. "How do you mean?"

"Maybe you can help me get over my shyness. You know, mentor me. Like I help you learn about childcare. And basic household maintenance."

Mentor her? At sex? That cold shower is going to have to be an ice bath now. "You keep saying things like that, and I'm going to stop finding reasons why it's a bad idea."

She swallows hard. I know she's trying to be brave when part of her really wants to fade back into the wallpaper. "Maybe the naughty babysitter and the bad daddy cliché could be hot? Like...if we just went with it?"

Oh man. My cock is going to bust the seam of these pants. "You want to role play?" Is she trying to be every fantasy I have right now?

"It would be fun, I think. To just disappear into a fantasy. Who are we hurting? We can't go on like this. I want to. With you. If you want to."

"You need to be sure. I can be a pretty dirty guy. I don't want to offend you or have things get weird between us."

"They don't have to be weird. Not if we decide now that they won't be. Neither of us can date other people right now. We don't have time. I certainly don't have the energy. But we can be...roommates with benefits, right?"

"Cassidy, I'm not joking about being dirty. I haven't gotten laid in six months. I'm going to be a pretty perverted fuck for your first time, I can guarantee it."

"Well, at least I'd have my first time."

Cherry. I can't believe I'm even contemplating this. Taking her virginity.

I take the towel she's twisting out of her hands. "Why that fantasy?" Because if she's suggesting it only because she thinks it will please me, then we are back to me manipulating her again. She's too important to me. To my girls. I need to be smart about this.

"It's hot?"

My expression must be pretty readable. If she can't talk about sex, we aren't having sex.

She twists her lips. "Conner, I'm always the responsible one. I want...I need...to not be in control. Even if it's just one night, I need someone, you, to take all the decisions away from me. I just want to feel. Not think."

"You want me to dominate you."

Please, God, say yes. Because I like taking charge in bed.

Instead, I get the deer in the headlights look.

Chapter Four

Cassidy

He takes a deep breath like he's about to say something. Then he changes his mind. "Good night, Cassidy."

Shit. Is that how I want this to go? "Wait." He pauses, but doesn't turn. I take a deep breath. Using a voice that's not quite mine and more or less jacked from a porno, I say, "You don't have to go, Mr. Webster. I thought you might like something else sweet. For your birthday."

He turns, eyebrows up. "That depends on what you're offering me, I guess."

I want to say something sexy. My tongue ties itself in a knot, though. Instead, I shoot for honesty. "I don't know how to do this. I'm not experienced. I'm afraid I'm doing this all wrong."

"Do you want me to help you right now?" He reaches his hand up and lightly, so lightly, traces my jaw with one finger.

"Yes," I whisper.

He tugs on my ponytail. "Tonight, Cassidy. I'll be Mr. Webster and you can be my shy, inexperienced babysitter. Would you like that?" He smiles. "I can see your pulse racing like crazy. I think you do like that. You can just relax, sweetness. Just submit to me. Can you do that? Can you trust me tonight to take you where you want to go?"

I hear a sound and realize it's me. Whimpering. "I think so."

"That's not good enough. Do you want to be my naughty babysitter tonight, yes or no?"

My pussy floods with moisture. I think it makes me a pervert, too, maybe. But I don't care. I want to play this game.

"Yes, Mr. Webster. I want to be your naughty babysitter tonight."

He swallows hard. "You change your mind, you tell me what your safe word is. Because as of right now, it isn't *no* and it isn't *stop*. In fact, *no* is just going to make me go at you harder. So, tell me a word that will halt the scene."

I didn't realize there was going to be a thinking portion of the game. "Um…"

"You're a smart girl. Tell me a safe word."

"Diaper," I blurt out. I should just retire now. I suck at being sexy.

He shakes his head, trying to hide his smile. "All right. That's the only thing that will stop me now. Do you understand? For the next few hours, you're not my partner. You're my shy teenage dream. And I'm not Conner. I'm the man you don't get to say no to. I'm the man who will take you where you've never been before. I'm going to make you so, so dirty. Got it, baby? You're not my friend tonight. You're not the woman who runs my house. You're going to learn what naughty is. You're my toy. You still on board? Do you think you can handle playing this role?"

I nod but I can't breathe. This is what I want. I want to give myself to him. Live the fantasy.

I don't know what to expect. Well, except I do. I've been watching a lot more porn this week. And all of it has been babysitter smut. I'm so turned on right now.

I've been reading some stories, too. I think Conner reads the same ones, maybe. Either that or he reached right into my head and pulled out my darkest desires. To be submissive to a dominating man. To let go. I'm not talking BDSM with props, but the idea of him controlling me makes me flush everywhere.

And I want to please him. I want to do this right. He's making it easy for me—all I have to do is play the shy, inexperienced teenaged babysitter. Which shouldn't be a character stretch.

"You've been a really good babysitter, Cassidy."

"Thank you, Mr. Webster."

He gets behind me, his hand on my hip and the rest of him brushing against my back.

I stiffen and try to scoot away, like my character would, but he pushes against me harder.

"Don't," I say. "It's not appropriate for you to touch me, Mr. Webster. I'm your babysitter." I don't know how I'm falling into this role-playing so easily but it's like a huge weight lifts off me. I'm not me, right now. It's letting go and becoming at the same time.

He squeezes me even harder, leaning in to speak in my ear so I feel his words as much as hear them. "Don't what, sweetness? Give my best babysitter a hug? I'm so grateful for the way you take care of things."

"You've been drinking, Mr. Webster."

He moves us a couple steps so I'm in front of the sink. "I like a beer or two at night. It helps relax me. What do you do to relax, sweetness?"

"You shouldn't be touching me." He's still squeezing me. I start to feel trapped. Mr. Webster is strong. Really strong. I'm falling into the game, and all my senses are leading me further in. I start to forget I'm playing. "I should be going since you're home now." He nuzzles my neck. I try to wrench away, but Mr. Webster holds me firm. "I have to go," I say.

"Do you like working here?"

"Yes."

"That's good. I'm glad. I want you to keep working for me, but I'm worried."

"Worried?"

"How do I know you're a good influence on the kids? How do I know you're a good girl?"

I feel like the script of a bad movie is on the teleprompter of my brain. "I am, Mr. Webster. I'm a very good girl."

"I don't know if I can believe you. You're going to have to convince me you're a good girl."

"What do you mean?"

"You need to prove to me you're a good influence, Cassidy. That you won't do something that would reflect badly on me as your employer. That I can trust you with my kids."

I think about what I could possibly say to convince him.

He takes a step back, and I sigh with relief. The adrenaline is coursing through me hard. "Tell me what you do when on your off time. What do you do with your friends?"

Ugh...what do normal girls do? It seems like it's been a really long time. "We watch movies and hang out."

"Are there boys there?"

I shrug. "Sometimes."

"Do you kiss the boys?"

My skin heats suddenly. "Mr. Webster, I don't want to talk about boys with you."

"That means yes."

"Yes, I've kissed boys before, but it's no big deal."

"Show me how you kiss the boys, then."

"What?" He can't mean it.

"Like this?" He pushes his mouth against mine. His lips are gentle, and he is kissing me almost sweetly. "Like that? Is that how you kiss them?"

I nod.

"That's not so bad."

I nod my head, agreeing with him. "You shouldn't be touching me like this, Mr. Webster. It's wrong."

"I'm just getting information. I have to know you're safe to have around my kids. That wasn't so bad, but do those boys ever do this?"

He pulls me to him again. This time, his clever tongue licks my lips until I open, allowing him in. His kiss is slow, his tongue tangling with mine languidly until all my muscles loosen. He tilts his head, deepening the kiss. He tastes like chocolate and coconut. All I am is sensation, the slow glide of his tongue, the rasp of stubble on his chin, the smells and tastes of him. My mind loosens more than my muscles, and I can't hold a thought. I've never been kissed into a hazy mind before, and he groans into my mouth.

He pulls back and goes for my throat. "Do you let them do that? Do you let the boys put their tongues in your mouth when you kiss them?" he asks against my skin.

"Sometimes," I whisper. Nothing like that. Never anything like that.

"Do they touch you here?" His hand gropes me, squeezing and kneading my breast.

I gasp loudly, surprised by the sudden change.

"Do they?"

My porno script opens back up. "My ex-boyfriend did, Mr. Webster. But we were going out for a long time before he tried."

"Over your bra or under, like this?" He snakes his hand under my T-shirt and into my bra, tweaking my nipple.

I know I shouldn't like it, know it is wrong. I can't believe I asked for this and I like it. My adrenaline is high, and I'm trembling.

"Under, but just once in a while. I swear."

"I'm not sure I believe you. Show me your tits, sweetness. I need to see something for certain."

He steps away, giving me room.

"Mr. Webster, I don't think..."

"Take off your shirt, Cassidy. Don't make me tell you again."

My breath catches in my throat. I should be scared. And I am. Kind of. Mostly, I am totally hot. I pull off my T-shirt, keeping my eyes on the floor. I don't need to look at my chest to know my nipples are pebbled like hard little stones in my bra.

"You're not done."

How far is this going to go? Are we really doing this? I shiver, remembering that veiny monster he keeps in his pants. I reach behind me and unclasp the bra, sliding the straps down and letting it fall to the floor.

"Those are real pretty, sweetness."

"Thank you," I whisper, not sure what to say while my boss stares at my breasts like they are a meal set before a starving man.

"Hold them up for me, baby. I want a really good look."

"I can't..." I'm so embarrassed.

"You want to keep this job, don't you?"

I nod.

"Tits. Now."

He's really good at this. He promised me a pervert and he's delivering.

I slide my hands beneath my breasts and cup them from below as if I were offering them to this older man I work for.

"Those are nice. Really nice." He leans down and licks one rock-hard nipple, causing a shockwave to course through my body straight to my pussy. Oh God. "You taste delicious. Anyone ever tell you that before?"

I shake my head.

He keeps his face by my tits, but looks up at me. "Are you saying no boy has ever licked your raspberry nips before?"

I shake my head again.

"I don't think I believe you. No boy has ever done this?" He licks the other one and then alternates between the two a few times.

I am going to pass out. I can't remember what is fact and what is fiction. I like it when he talks roughly, when he treats me like an object. What does that say about me?

But he likes it, too. And we're adults. Lonely adults with too many responsibilities. We're not hurting anyone. We're just getting off.

"Mr. Webster, we're being so bad."

He puts his hands on my hips and sucks my left nipple all the way into his mouth, and I groan out loud with pleasure.

He steps back, and the cool air hits the warm saliva he left behind on my boob. "Just because nobody has sucked them before doesn't make you innocent." He reaches for my hand and sets it on his groin. "You ever touch your boyfriends here?"

"No," I whisper, my voice gone who knows where. He forces my hand to rub him through his sweats. He is so hard and big. I clear my throat. "We shouldn't be doing this. It's wrong."

He's watching my face very carefully. Since I'm not pulling my hand back, he knows I'm still playing along.

"Don't you want to see what you've been missing, sweetness?" He takes my hand and shoves it down his pants. His pubic hair crinkles around my hand, and he strokes my fingers down his shaft. It feels different than I thought it would. Like steel encased in velvet.

Desire spears through me. I feel so naughty.

He tips his head back as if in ecstasy. "You know how long I've been waiting for this?"

"Mr. Webster, please let me go. You don't want to make me do this."

"Baby, you have been begging to do this for months. You think I don't notice you checking out my cock? Did you like watching me the other night?"

I blush even hotter. Now he's bringing reality back in. This weird mix of the real Cassidy and the naughty babysitter Cassidy are turning into one.

He pulls my hand out and circles both my wrists in one powerful grip. He backs me away from the sink and against the wall. He raises my arms above my head so my tits lift, pinning my hands to the wallpaper. I groan as he plunges his other hand beneath the waistband of my shorts and into my panties.

He traces one finger down my slit, and I shudder, looking into his eyes as he grins like the devil. "You're soaking wet. All for me, sweetness." He thrums his thumb against my clit, and I bow my back, arching my pussy to him. "Your boyfriends ever touch you here?"

He pushes my button again, and I gasp. "No. Just you. You're the only one."

"That's a good girl. You waited so Mr. Webster could show you what you really want. What you really need. Isn't that right?" He pushes a finger into me and presses my clit with his thumb.

"Oh God," I cry.

"Jesus, baby, you're going to fucking come in my hand."

He keeps diddling me, and I become desperate. He is going to make me come. I should stop him, at least pretend to, but what he is doing feels so fucking good. I hit my head on the wall trying to knock some sense back in, but then he lowers his head and starts sucking on my tits again, and I know I am going to lose.

"Please, Mr. Webster. Stop this. Please."

"You're so fucking wet right now that it's running down your leg." He slows down but doesn't take his hand away. I don't think my legs will hold out much longer. "Those boys you kissed weren't man enough to let your inner woman out, but I am, sweetness. I'm all man. What you need. An older man. A very bad daddy."

He pulls his hand out of my pussy, and I almost cry with disappointment. He wipes his fingers on my nipple and then sucks the juices off. The sensation makes me clench my legs together. "You taste like honey."

He lets go of my wrists and steps back.

I am free, but I don't know what to do.

While I am trying to decide my next move, he reaches for the hem of his tank top and pulls it over his head. Oh God. He's perfect like a statue. Like the cover of every romance book I've ever read. I want to touch him. That tattoo mesmerizes me. I want all of him pressed against me. He raises his eyebrows like he can read my thoughts as he pushes down his sweats.

I need to get back on script. "What...what are you doing, Mr. Webster?" I ask, even as he kicks the last of his clothing off.

And there it is.

The beast that lives in his pants. It is stiff as a flagpole and pointing just as proudly. I can't tear my eyes from it.

His hand goes to his cock, and he pumps it slowly.

"Right here? You're going to do that right here?" I am trapped between him and the wall.

And I can't tear my eyes off his dick.

"Did you like the way my dick felt in your hand, Cassidy? I know you did. I like the way you feel too, all slick and moist and hot." His eyes are hooded, and he focuses on my tits. "And the way your pussy tastes. Damn. I just got a small sample, and I'll never forget how sweet you were."

I can't get a deep breath. His words are hypnotizing me to the movements of his hand on his cock. It has to be eight or nine inches. But it is the girth that really amazes me.

He isn't pounding it fast. He takes his time, stroking up and down slowly, his eyes on my tits. I clench my pussy tightly to keep from humping the air. I want to dip my fingers in and come so badly.

He picks up my hand, and I don't pull it back when he brings it to his stiff cock. He folds my fingers around him as far as they will go, and moves my fist up and down in the same rhythm he was using before.

"There, that's not so bad, is it? You're doing so good, baby. That feels great."

He loosens his grip, but I don't let go. My hand slips a little on the pre-cum oozing out, and it helps me to slide my hand faster. "Like this, Mr. Webster?"

"Mmmm," he says, reaching his hands to my tits again.

He strokes them softly, and I add my other hand to his cock. His strokes become harder until he is pinching my nipples just like I do to myself sometimes. I cry out as a tiny orgasm rips through me, stunning me. I didn't know I could come without touching my pussy.

He chuckles and loosens me off his cock. "That's what I thought."

Before I know what is happening, he grasps my waist and picks me up as if I weigh only a few ounces. He plops me onto the counter and spreads my legs wide, pushes the crotch of my shorts to the side, and dives his tongue into my slit.

Up and down, in and out. He uses his whole face in my pussy, making noises like some kind of animal. Tonguing me, nipping me. I have to rest the backs of my knees on his shoulders and hold on to his hair as he goes crazy on my clit. The pressure inside me is building higher and higher as I squirm against his face. I can't stop my body from arching and trembling.

"Come on my face, Cassidy," he says into my pussy. "Get it all over me."

I have no choice but to obey. The biggest orgasm I've ever had rips through me, ricocheting off every nerve. He is down there slurping me, moaning about how good I taste, and still I can't stop humping his mouth.

I am a shaky mess when he finally lifts his head. Mr. Webster grabs the back of my head and pulls me into a kiss I shouldn't want. I try to back away.

"Taste how good you are," he says and thrusts his tongue into my mouth again, forcing my own musky sweetness into my mouth.

Incredibly, it turns me on more, the taste of me on his tongue, and I suck on him, unable to stop myself.

He rips my shorts down and wraps my legs around his waist, pulling me easily off the countertop. His turgid dick grazes my bottom and makes me squirm as he carries me. "Which bed should I fuck you in, sweetness?"

Oh God. My breasts rub against his chest. "No, Mr. Webster...We can't—" but the motion of his cock under me as he takes us upstairs is getting me hot again, distracting me.

He lays me on the bed, his, and goes back to eating out my pussy.

I come again, hard. I'm wrung out and shaking.

That's when he says, "Diaper."

Chapter Five

Conner

Cassidy scrambles up and away from me. She's flushed and sexy as hell. I want her like breath, but this isn't right.

"What?" she cries. "What did you just say? Did you just use *my* safe word?"

"Easy, sweetness." I put my hands on her legs, but she moves them away.

Fuck, her shiny eyes are killing me. "Did I do something wrong? Why don't you want me?"

"That's just it. I do want you. You, Cassidy. You're the sexiest woman I've ever been with, but I don't want you to pretend you're someone else. Not our first time."

"I don't understand. I thought...the role playing..."

I come up to the front of the bed and pull her head onto my chest. She's stiff and uncomfortable, and I'm aware that I probably ruined the mood for good. "The role playing was good. It was really good." Fuck. Watching her come. Hearing her come. Finally tasting that pussy that has been haunting my dreams. Good doesn't do justice to it. "But our first time together...I don't want it to be a game. I don't want you to be playing a part. I want *you*. Just you."

"I'm not sure I understand."

"I think you do."

"Conner..."

"You're sexy and perfect. Just the way you are. And I don't want you to need to feel like I'm tricking you out of your virginity for you to feel like it's okay. I thought I could handle it, but I can't. I want to fuck you, but I want more."

"More?"

"I'll teach you every damn thing you want to know about sex, Cassidy. But you need to call me Conner. Maybe after we've had sex a hundred times, we can play some games. But I want to be real with you. With us."

"I don't know what to say. I feel like you're rejecting me."

"I'm not. I swear." I roll her over onto her back. "I want to make this good for you, Cass. Will you let me? As me? Not some asshole taking something he shouldn't?"

"Why are you doing this? If you don't want me, just say so."

"I do want you. I want you so much I can hardly stay in my own skin right now. You're killing me."

She bites that lip, undoing me. "I know I'm not sexy."

"That's a goddamn lie." I place her hand on my rock-hard cock.

Her hand strokes it softly, and I shiver under her inexperienced touch. "You really think I'm sexy?"

"I can prove it."

She's quiet and the stroking stops. "Will you still be dominating and take control?"

"Fuck yeah, I will."

She nods, but her eyes are laser focused on mine. That's what we were missing downstairs. This connection.

It's better. So much better.

"Do you know how many times I've already made you come tonight?"

She shakes her head. "I lost the ability to do math when we were in the kitchen, Conner."

There's my girl. I chuckle into her chest. That's what I missed. That sense of humor. That sense she's really with me.

"I love making you come. It's my favorite hobby now. I hope you enjoy it because it's nonstop orgasms for you from now on. Once those girls are asleep, you're mine. Every night." She whimpers when I take her tit into my mouth again. "I loved it when you came just from me on your tits. That ever happen to you before?"

I bite down gently, causing her answer of, "No," to turn into a squeal of pleasure.

"I think I'm going to start keeping a journal of your orgasms, sweetness. All the ways I can make you come. What makes you squeak and what makes you scream." I rub her with my whole body, the friction of her soft skin against the bottom of my shaft is the sweetest torture. "I'm going to find every place on your body that makes you shiver. I'm going to make you so, so dirty."

She arches her back reflexively. "That seems like a full-time job, Conner."

"Oh, it is. It's also going to take a long time. I hope you weren't thinking you'd get off on my dick tonight and that'd be it. I've got a lot of research I want to do."

I dip my fingers into her pussy. She's wet. God, so wet.

"More than tonight then?" she asks.

"Cassidy, you fucking own me now."

She raises up on her elbows, her eyes wide with surprise. I get two fingers in her tight sheath, stretching her, and find the spot I'm looking for. "Conner!" she cries out.

"Yeah, that's it." She doesn't look away from me, from this connection. "I mean it. I'll dominate the fuck out of you in this bedroom, but you own me." I knew it the minute she lit that candle this morning. I should have known it months ago. But it was forged on my soul the second I got a taste of her on my tongue.

Her legs start shaking and she starts coming on my hand. That one is going in the journal for sure. Under the letter G. My girl has an easy-to-find spot, thank God.

My dick is leaking pre-cum all over the bed, and I don't want to lose my whole load there, so it's time. I don't take my hands off Cassidy while I reach across the bed and into the drawer. She's still shaking and coming down, so I don't want to break contact. I take a good look at that pussy while I'm rolling on the condom. You'd think that the twins would be excellent incentive for birth control, but as my eyes skim up Cassidy's body, I'm mentally putting a baby inside her.

Fuck, she'd be gorgeous. Round and fertile. And the idea of filling her with cum makes me leak even more. But she and the girls are my top priority, and right now, a pregnancy wouldn't be good for any of them.

Someday, though.

I can't believe I'm even thinking about someday. Just this morning, I had no thoughts other than just getting through the days one at a time. Now I'm planning a future and mentally breeding the poor girl the night she loses her virginity.

I part her pussy lips with my cock and slide up and down her slit, getting juicy and lubed up while I tease her. Damn, she feels good. I can't wait to get inside. I drag my cock across her clit that's peeking out of its hood, and she throws her head back. She's so pretty as she lets go. I tap the head of my cock on that clit a few times and then go back to spreading her juices around, using the tip of my dick around her entrance.

She raises up on her elbows again and gets a good look at what I'm doing and looks a little scared.

"It's never going to fit."

I swear my cock pulses at her words. Yeah, it's gonna be a tight squeeze, all right. I push the tip in and pause, letting her stretch around my head, and then push a little further. "You feel amazing. Your pussy is grabbing my cock like a vise."

I push it in a little more and I see stars. I've already filled up her little pussy, and I'm barely in. I tear my gaze away from where we are joined and notice she's kinda pale. Not good. I need to get her back on board, fast. She likes dirty talk and when I tell her what to do, so I'll give us both what she wants.

"Look at it. Look at my cock filling you up. Your little pussy is creaming for it. Watch it take my whole cock, Cassidy. Look at us."

She moans.

"You like that, sweetness? You're such a good girl. You're gonna take all of my cock, aren't you?" I put my thumb on her clit, giving it a little pressure. "You might be a good girl to the rest of the world, but in this room, you can be a very bad girl."

She whimpers in disappointment when I pull out a little.

"Oh yeah, that's my girl. You want your cock back, don't you? Do you want to be my naughty girl? Do you want to take all this cock?"

She bites her lip and moans.

"Say it," I order her.

"Yes. Yes, please. I want to be a bad girl."

Fuck. Me. Hearing those words from her sweet lips makes it hard not to come right now. With her admission ringing in my ears, I push the rest of the way inside her, leaning over her to take her gasp of shock with a kiss. I'm holding absolutely still below my neck and it's killing me, but she needs to adjust, so I focus on kissing her, distracting her with my tongue. Her nails are digging into my shoulders, and I feel like a real shit for causing her pain. I kiss her and when she starts responding again, I start kissing her the way my dick wants to fuck her. After about minute, she relaxes her body, but her pussy is still so tight it's almost hurting *me*.

"I don't want to hurt you, sweetness. I want to make this so good for you." I start slow, my thrusts shallow and even. "You okay? Tell me what you're feeling right now."

"Full. I feel so full. But the pinch is going away."

I use two fingers on her clit and roll it in a circular motion. "That's good, baby."

The sight of my glistening shaft easing in and out of her beautiful body has the cum churning in my balls. But I can't go yet. Not until she does.

I'm going to make this girl come around my cock if it's the last thing I do on this fucking planet. I start fucking her faster, thrusting my hard cock deep inside her warm pussy and filling her up with each stroke. My cock is pushing deep with each urgent thrust.

I can't believe I'm finally inside her after all these months of yearning for her. "You're definitely a dirty girl now, Cassidy. I've never wanted to come so bad in my life. All because of you. Do you want me to come?

"Oh God, yes. I want you to come inside me."

"That's a good girl. I need you to do something for me, sweetness."

"Anything, Conner."

My name from her mouth ratchets my lust up another notch.

"Play with your tits while I fuck you."

She looks confused for a minute, but her hands come up automatically to her breasts and she starts tweaking her nipples.

"Pinch them," I order her and I fuck her roughly, my strong hands digging into her thick hips to hold her still while I push my rod deeper and deeper. "Harder, Cassidy."

She's into her nipple play, and it isn't long before my strokes and her pinches take her where I want her. Mindless. Shaking. Moaning. She tightens around my cock, milking me while she does this sexy mewing noise. I grab her arms off her tits and pin them on the pillow on either side of her head, diving in to kiss her just as my body tightens. I roar into her mouth and explode in her pussy harder than I've ever come before, my girl writhing beneath me.

The spasms take me someplace I've never been. Heaven, I guess. And now that I've found it, you can be damn sure I'll never leave it.

My fingers entwine with hers, and I pull back to look at her. At the face I vow I'll wake up next to for the rest of my life. "You're mine, Cassidy."

She nods. "Say it."

"I'm yours, Conner."

I need to get off her—I'm probably crushing her. I need to dispose of the condom. I need to get a warm washcloth and tend to this sweet woman, who's probably sore.

But for a few seconds more, I need this. Her eyes on mine. Me still inside her. I can't find the words, but everything is different now.

Chapter Six

Cassidy

We're just finishing cleaning the kitchen when the doorbell rings. Conner and I shoot each other questioning looks. Nobody comes here. Like ever. Which is fine. We've had three weeks of blissful lovemaking, and I was looking forward to another night of the same. The girls are asleep, I have no homework, and Conner promised me a massage.

Conner opens the front door, and three men stroll in carrying beer and bags of chips.

"We figured you were in need of a poker night, dude," one says. He nods a hello to me, and they start setting up around the dining table, talking and joking as if this were an everyday occurrence.

"Uh, guys?" Conner says. "It's really not a good night."

"C'mon, man. You haven't been out with us in seven months. We won't wake the kids. We'll even leave by ten." He puts the case of beer down and turns to me. "I'm Deacon." He holds out his hand, which I shake while looking at Conner.

"Cassidy this is Deacon, Charlie, and Matt. Guys this is Cassidy. She's..." He looks at me with new eyes. "She's the nanny."

I don't know what I was expecting him to say. I am the nanny, after all. That doesn't stop the feeling that I'd just swallowed an ice cube, and it's freezing everything inside me as it slides down my throat.

My heart especially.

The last three weeks have been amazing, but we didn't put labels on it. It seemed too new to sully with expectations. We just built a cocoon around the house and pretended there wasn't an outside world.

But there is. And it's in the cocoon with us now.

Conner is looking at me like he's seen a ghost. Or maybe he's just seeing the writing on the wall like I am.

I'm the nanny.

Of course, I am.

I'm the teen babysitter.

What seemed so right ten minutes ago now seems sordid. Wow, when reality crashes your party, it does with the finesse of the Kool-Aid Man crashing through a wall.

"I'll finish cleaning in the kitchen. You should visit with your friends. When I'm done, I'll head...home...and be back first thing in the morning."

Conner closes his eyes. Deacon says, "Wait. Cassidy? Could you stay longer? I'll pay you whatever Conner does. That way if the kids wake up, he can still hang out for a while."

Conner says nothing. Nothing. I'm starting to feel sick that I get paid to do what I do. Am I getting paid to sleep with my boss?

I blink back my epiphany. That's for Future Cassidy to think about. Right now, getting away from all these people is goal number one. "Yeah, sure. I'll bring the baby monitor into the guest room and study in there."

I feel Conner's eyes on me as I go into the kitchen, but he's still said zero.

It was actually easier in the living room, when all my insides were iced over. Now that I'm alone, I feel the prickles of a thaw coming. It hurts. I want the numb back.

We had pretty much finished the kitchen, so I rinse out the sink and towel dry it so I at least feel busy.

"Cassidy."

I don't turn around from the sink. I *can't*. "There's still some dip in the fridge, if you want to have it with your chips."

"Cassidy," Conner repeats.

I squeeze my eyes closed. *Not now. Not now. You can't break yet. Just a few more minutes.*

His hands are on my hips now. His chest to my back. "I didn't mean to hurt your feelings."

"I'm fine."

"I didn't know what you wanted me to tell them. I didn't want to put you in an awkward position."

"You didn't."

He wraps his arms around my middle and rests his chin on my shoulder. "You think I can't tell that you're hurting right now? You think I don't care that I'm the one that did it?"

"I'm fine. You should go back out there. They might come looking for you. We don't want them to suspect."

"I don't care if they do. Sweetness, you know you're more than the nanny to me, right?"

I don't answer because I know I'm more than the nanny when we're in bed. But I don't know what I am when the real world rings the doorbell. These guys have seen him date a lot of women. It probably never even occurred to them that he could be having sex with me. They probably can't even remember what I look like already. I'm the wallflower. I forgot it for these weeks. I remember it now. With all my other insecurities.

"Cassidy." His voice is low, gravelly near my ear. An unwanted warmth rushes to my center. *Damn it.*

I exhale and squeeze his hands. "I'm fine, Conner. Go have a nice time."

His mouth is still near my ear, his breath hot against the sensitive skin there. "I'd rather stay in here with you." He nuzzles my neck. "I love the way you smell."

"Conner."

"Let's tell them."

"Tell them what? That the dorky girl next door has a crush on you? That your nanny takes care of your kids all day and then takes care of your dick at night? What exactly are we going to tell them?"

He goes stiff and steps back like it burned to touch me.

I turn. "I'm sorry."

But it's too late. His jaw is squared in repressed anger. His posture is tight. But his eyes are wounded.

"Conner, I'm sorry."

He stares at me for a long time. I bite my lip, swallowing the golf ball trying to move up my throat. But I can't stop the tear.

"Shit, that's not fair," he says. He pulls me into his arms. "Please don't cry. I can deal with a lot of things, but making you cry is not one of them."

It feels good in his arms. Too good. I want this. I want the life we've been playing these past three weeks. I want him to be mine. But the fact is, when pressed, neither of us knew how to introduce me, and that is the first ding in the windshield, I think. It's weaker now. Ready to crack. If our first instinct was to hide our relationship, then maybe no matter how good it feels, it isn't right.

Just like that first night, we've been role playing all along.

And if it isn't right, then there are two people we need to put ahead of our selfish desire. The sleeping babies upstairs. They can't afford for us to play house and wreck their lives. If we break up after they are used to us, then they lose all their stability again.

I pull back, put on an awkward grin. "You deserve a night of fun with the guys. But I think it's best that I go home tonight." I hand him the baby monitor. "They probably won't wake up, but just in case."

"Cassidy, don't do this."

"I'm not doing anything. My mom has been bugging me to hang out for a while now. I'll be back before you go to work in the morning."

"Cass—"

I hold my hand up. "Diaper."

The safe word. The one that means stop.

He wasn't expecting that. His face goes slack with shock.

I run out the back door. I don't have shoes. I don't have my laptop or my books. And I certainly don't have my dignity.

In my childhood room, I pull back my curtains and look across the lawns into the room I haven't slept in for weeks at Conner's house. It was only a month ago that I was on that side, wishing I were at home. Now, this doesn't feel like home. Not anymore. But home isn't next door, either. It's always been temporary. The plan had always been to get a permanent nanny.

My heart breaks because I think it's time.

There is money for it. The house is paid for and there was money left from the life insurance policies. Conner met with a financial advisor about a month after the funeral. He made sure the bulk of the money got put away for the girls—but there is a budget for a nanny. I didn't take the full amount he offered, but someone else will. Maybe they'll even take room and board.

That sends an arrow of fire to my gut. Thinking of someone else living there. Taking care of the girls. Tucking them in at night. Giving them their baths. Watching them sleep.

That's how I know it's time. If I feel like this now—how bad will it hurt two years from now? Four?

I've spent the last few months sort of hand-waving over my feelings because everything felt right. But what happens when it doesn't? When Conner meets a woman he's attracted to who's old enough to go to a bar? What happens to me when the girls are in school all day? Do I become Alice from *The Brady Bunch*? Will I get a room off the kitchen while everyone around me has a life of their own?

I can't regret loving all three of them. But nobody can move on if I stay. And I don't want to just be the nanny. I want it all. I may never find it, but pretending isn't going to work forever.

The next morning is awkward. We're overly polite. He's cleaned up after his party, something he wouldn't have thought to do six months ago. He's watching me very carefully as I feed the girls breakfast. He automatically refills my coffee, putting the right amount of sugar in my cup, and my mouth goes dry because I know I have to leave. The temptation to stay is too strong.

I hand Conner a sheet of paper. "Before you go to work, do you think you could look these over?"

He glances at it. "What is this?"

"My job description and possible ads. I thought I would contact the agencies today. It's time you found a permanent solution. We talked about it a few months ago, remember? That I was just temporary until things got under control?"

Conner says nothing. His hand curls into a fist, crinkling the paper, and he kisses the girls' heads before he strides out the door.

I'm glad for once that the girls are such good distractions because they keep me too busy all morning to wallow in all my angsty feelings.

At one o'clock, I take Ashley to the doctor for a possible ear infection. My mom stayed with Hayden, so I take advantage of having just one baby and stop at Target on the way home. I pull into the parking lot, open my door, and see the gun first, the man holding it second.

Chapter Seven

Conner

I've been shitty to everyone at work today, and I can't work up the fucks to care about it.

Last night, my first night without Cassidy in the house with me in a long time, was horrible, but it was a picnic compared to finding out she wants out permanently.

Yeah, okay. I blew it by introducing her as the nanny. I'm not ashamed of her. Of us. But it's complicated and not something I wanted to discuss with my idiot friends before I've discussed it with Cassidy.

And at the first sign of trouble, she's out.

Right. Okay. That's not fair. There have been lots of signs of trouble over the last seven months, and she hasn't bailed. She's stuck by me through everything. She's been the person that kept me tethered to the planet when gravity was gone.

So how can she just leave me now? Am I so easy to leave? Are the girls? I thought she loved them. I thought we were building something. None of it makes sense.

She's only eighteen.

I try to remember what I was like at that age. I should cut her some slack. She should be going to parties and having fun. Maybe I really am a selfish bastard. Have I been trying to mold her? Manipulate her? Maybe I should have known better. Pushed her away. Maybe after some time has passed, I'll realize that I was using her, even if I didn't mean to. That I was blinded by the pretty girl and the convenience of having a ready-made mom for my girls and a wife for my house.

Wife.

Fuck.

I love her. I want to *marry* her. Those feelings I had the first time we made love were real. She's mine. I say that to her every time we fuck—but I guess I never say it when we have clothes on. How would she know how I feel if I don't tell her? She probably thinks the things I say about her being mine are just sex talk.

I have screwed this up. Bad. Maybe she's right. Maybe we'd all be better off if she moved out. She needs to be free. Have fun. I'll find a nice grandma-like nanny for the girls. I'll concentrate on being a good dad. Things will be fine.

Yeah. No, they won't. I want to rage at the world. This is why I never let myself get close to anyone before. I'm not cut out for loving and losing.

I see Deacon approaching. He looks nervous. I don't blame him, I've been biting off everyone's head.

"Hey man, I need to talk to you," he says.

"Not a good time, Deacon."

I turn back to my work, but he grabs my arm. I get a good look at his face and my world bottoms out again for the second time in less than a year. I know that look. That's the same one that was on the cop's face when he told me Sandy died.

"No," I say. The world starts spinning. My mouth tastes like copper. "No, no, no, no."

"There's been an accident." He clutches me so I don't go down. "Ashley and Cassidy were in a car..." My vision tunnels. I hear hospital and stable and something about a ride.

"Where's Hayden?"

"She's at the house. Cassidy's mom was watching her, but she wants to be at the hospital with her daughter, so my mom is on the way over. Is that okay, man? You've met my mom, right? She'll take care of the baby. I'll go over after and help her, okay?"

I nod. Still not processing. Bits and pieces come to me on the ride to the hospital. I remember Ashley had a doctor's appointment. I remember the way the girls' hair smelled this morning. I remember not even saying goodbye to Cassidy because I was so pissed off. My heart seizes.

Fate can't be this cruel, right? I try to be a good guy. I never meant to hurt anyone. Is this my punishment? For wanting Cassidy? For taking her? Is God going to take her and Ashley from me in retribution?

I burst through the hospital doors and slide on the polished floor when I take a corner too fast.

I see her. Cassidy.

Something loosens over my heart. She's not dead. I wheeze in a breath.

Cassidy is standing in the hall in a hospital issued gown and robe arguing with a nurse. She's bruised and bandaged and beautiful. God, she's so beautiful.

I run to her, and she collapses in my arms. "It's okay, sweetness. I got you." I want to squeeze her into me, but I don't know her injuries. I don't know how badly she's been hurt. "Ashley?"

"They won't tell me anything."

Because she's the nanny. Not family.

Of course.

I look at the nurse. "I'm Ashley's father." I think that's the first time I've ever said it out loud. "Cassidy is the only mother Ashley knows. You have my permission to tell her anything about Ashley that you would tell me." I notice Cassidy's mom in the corridor. She's staring at me as I hold her girl, and I can read on her face that she *knows*.

And that is fine.

I focus on the nurse again. "Please tell us what's going on with our daughter."

Cassidy

AS SOON AS I FOUND out Ashley was stable and they let us see her, I pretty much passed out. They got me to my room, put something in my IV and that's all I remember.

Now I'm staring at a spot on the wall trying to focus. The room is dark, and I have no idea what time it is. Everything hurts and I'm queasy.

"You awake?"

I startle. The jolt does not feel good. "Conner," I croak out. He gives me a sip of water through a straw, easing my throat. "I didn't know you were here; you startled me. Where's Ashley?"

"She's fine. Sleeping."

"What about Hayden?"

"Would you relax and stop worrying? She's fine. Everyone is fine. It's you we're worried about." He turns on a light, and I blink at the brightness. "Sorry." He sits next to the bed and takes my hand in his. "How are you feeling, Cass?"

"Worse than those three days the girls kept us up every night with the flu."

He smiles and his eyes are soft. "You gave me a scare. Do you remember what happened?"

Every time I start to think about this afternoon, my mind closes off. "Not really."

Our fingers entwine. "You saved Ashley."

I close my eyes against the memory of the gun. "He pulled me out of the car."

His grip tightens. "I know. The witnesses say he threw you to the ground." Conner's voice cracks on the last word, so he clears his throat. "But you got up and chased the car."

"He had Ashley. I couldn't let him take Ashley."

I'm blinking against the tears when the bed shifts and Conner is next to me, holding me close. "I was so scared. When they told me there was an accident...it was like Sandy all over again. But you're okay." He's stroking my hair like I'm a cat. "You were so brave."

"I caused the accident. When he was trying to get me off the door handle, he swerved and hit the—"

"Sweetness, you got our girl away from him. You did the right thing. And she doesn't even have a bruise. They just want to watch her tonight." He shifts in the bed to give me more room. "You need to rest."

I don't think there is any way I'll fall asleep, but my eyelids are so heavy. When I blink, it's morning and I'm alone with the nurse.

And my mother.

"We'll be back in a bit with your discharge papers, Cassidy. Your mom brought you fresh duds to change into, but go slow, okay? You don't want to overdo it."

When she leaves, my mom is looking at me funny. "Are you going to tell me what's been going on in that house all these months?"

"Mom, it's not like that."

"Please, it's exactly like that. I saw the way you were looking at him. Cassidy, he's too old for you. He's using you. Think about it. Why would a man his age want a teenager?"

"Thanks for the vote of confidence, Mom." I ease my feet to the floor. "It's not what you think."

"I think he should be ashamed of himself. First, for seducing a young girl and second for using you like a convenience."

"Mom, stop. He's not using me. I get paid to take care of the girls."

"And to take care of his needs? Cassidy, please. You're a smart girl."

I stand slowly. Everything in my body hurts. "Do you know if Ashley is being discharged today, too?"

"Let Conner worry about Ashley. I'm taking you home, and we are going to have a very long talk. He needs to find a new sitter. My daughter is not for sale."

"Mom!"

"I love her."

I whip my head to the door where Conner is standing, and then the world goes kind of sideways. I don't know why the floor is moving until Conner catches me. He and my mom ease me back to the bed, and she goes to get a nurse.

"You okay?" he asks, pushing my hair off my face.

"I just moved my head too fast."

The nurse comes in to check me over, and my mom is shooting daggers at Conner, and all I can think about is that he said he loves me. When the nurse leaves, declaring that I will have to be careful and be with someone for the next few days, I grasp Conner's hand.

"Did you mean it?"

"Of course, I meant it."

My heart feels so full. "You never said...I wasn't sure..."

He looks at my mom. She's got her arms crossed over her chest and looks like she's plotting seven ways to kill him and what she'll do with his body.

"Mom, can you give us a minute please?"

She glares, but leaves the room.

"Look, if you still want me to get a new nanny, I understand. But I'm hoping you'll give us chance, even if you don't stay at the house. Maybe we can date or something. I don't know how that would work, but I need you in my life."

I'm not sure if the world is pitching because of what he's telling me or not. I hold on to his hand. "I love you, too. I don't want to quit. If you still want me."

He smiles and kisses me gently, very gently. "We'll make it work. It sounds like I need a temp nanny, though. You need some time off."

"No, I want to take care of the babies...I..."

"Cass?"

I hear my name, but it's so far away. The drums are beating so loudly. Wait. Drums? I think it's my heart...it's all I can hear. The room gets dark. Very, very dark.

Chapter Eight

Conner

If there were a rug in the corridor of the hospital, I'd have worn through it with my pacing. I'm waiting for them to bring her back from her labs.

Instead of pacing the halls, her mom sits statue still on the chair outside her room. She's white as a ghost and gripping the handles of her purse like it's all that's keeping her on the planet. Like she doesn't trust gravity.

I can't lose Cassidy. I just can't. I want to run down the halls and smash things. I stop at the end of the hall. I've passed it about a hundred times, but this time, I enter the chapel.

I sit in the chair, but don't pray. I just sit. A few minutes later, I'm not alone. Cassidy's mom sits next to me.

"How long?"

"How long what?"

"How long have you been taking advantage of my daughter?"

I can't even work up anger. I'd be pissed as hell if I were in her shoes, too. "We've been together about three weeks, ma'am. But I realize that I've been taking advantage of her kindness since the night of the accident. She's the one who has kept the family together, not me. I didn't know anything about kids. She's an amazing woman."

"Girl," she corrects me. "She's an amazing girl. You say you love her."

"Yes."

"You know she's too young for you. That she'll throw away her youth on you. Taking care of your house and your kids and sacrificing her own life. If you love her, maybe you will think about putting her first. Maybe you'll think of letting her go."

"You think that would be best for her."

She isn't really looking at me. Just straight ahead with a soft focus. "I know it would be best for her. And so do you."

It might very well be.

"I won't make decisions for her. Because she's mature enough to know what she wants. If she wants to go, I won't stop her. But don't ask me to stop loving her, because I will never do that. Whether she's with me or not, I love her."

She swings her head at me, searching my eyes for what, I'm not sure. "We should get back out there, in case she comes back."

This time, I sit next to her on the chairs outside the room. And we wait.

Chapter Nine

Cassidy

This time, when they discharge me, it's for real. I didn't have an embolism. I didn't have a worsening concussion. I didn't have any of the horrible things they suspected.

I have a baby. Inside me. One that I haven't told anyone about.

So far, they think the baby is okay. I'm afraid that they are wrong. And every time I close my eyes, I see that gun. I'm sort of a mess.

My mom takes me home, puts me in my room. I don't fight her and neither does Conner.

For two days.

He told me he loved me. I want to believe him. I really do. I know I love him. But what will he say about a baby? Life is already so chaotic. How do we add another baby to this now?

I'm worried about Ashley. And I miss sweet little Hayden, too.

I'm sitting in my dad's recliner watching *Mean Girls* for the hundredth time in my life when my mom pops her head in.

"Conner is here."

My hands go to my tummy automatically, earning me a "your gig is up" look from my mom, but she doesn't say anything.

I pause the movie and then turn off the TV. It feels silly, watching that movie right now. Girlish.

Maybe I am too young for all of this.

"Hey."

He looks good. Too good. He steals my breath as he crosses the room and kisses the top of my head gently. He's got some bags under his eyes. I hope he's been eating real food. Maybe he went back to frozen pizzas and beer in the days we've been apart. Maybe it's not my business.

He sits awkwardly on the couch. "Are you okay? I thought you would call or come over or…"

I play with the ends of the quilt on my lap. "I'm sorry. I've been sleeping a lot."

The way he's concentrating so fiercely on my face makes my eye twitch.

"What's really going on?"

"Nothing."

He winces. "Right. Nothing. You're only avoiding me and the girls. No big deal."

"Conner, I'm not avoiding you. I'm just resting."

"I don't understand what changed. I thought, in the hospital, when I told you I loved you…"

"I'm pregnant."

God, did I really just blurt that out like that?

Conner's face goes slack with shock. "You're pregnant?"

I nod.

"That's why you're avoiding me?"

"I'm not—okay, maybe I am. I needed a little time to figure out how I feel."

He's biting the inside of his cheek. He reminds me of a tiger pacing its cage. All that energy tightly coiled and waiting for the opportunity to make a break for it. "We used protection."

I massage the spot where I imagine the baby is twirling around. "Nothing is foolproof."

Leaning back against the cushions, he rubs his face. "Wow. God, every time I was inside you, part of me fantasized about putting a baby in there, but I never thought we'd really do it."

Wait, what? "You *fantasized* about getting me pregnant?"

He blinks at me like he hadn't realized that was weird to say out loud until just now. "It was, I don't know, a primal thing I guess. Biology."

"Well, um, surprise! Biology won."

Why am I being so snarky? It's not his fault. Or not only his fault anyway.

"So how do you feel, Cassidy? You've had some time to think without me now."

I wish I knew how I felt. I know the right thing for everyone is probably not for me to be pregnant. But I love the baby already. How could I not? I love its father. I love its siblings. "It's not a good time for a baby." I choke out the words because they are true, but they hurt.

Conner pales, and then his face gets red. "You don't think I can handle it, do you? That's why you kept it to yourself. Were you going to decide without me?"

"No, of course not. I'm not worried about you. You're a great dad. But what if I'm not ready to be a mom?"

He laughs and looks around the room like he's expecting a cameraman to jump out from behind a piece of furniture. "Seriously? Cass, what do you think you've been doing for the last seven months if not being a mom?"

"I'm just the nanny."

He narrows his gaze at me. "Do not say that. We both know that is not true."

"Well, okay. But we've only been together a few weeks. Conner, we haven't even been on a date. We're not ready to parent."

"Sweetness, we've been *living* together for seven months, but I have no problem taking you out on a date if that makes you feel better." He pauses. "What's really going on? We do pretty well at parenting together, and you already know that. What really has you so worried?"

"Everything."

"All right. Let's make a list of everything and then we'll tackle it one at a time. That's what you do, right? Make lists?"

There are literally lists in every room of that house. Yes, I make lists. But he's not supposed to be the reasonable one in this situation. He's supposed to be freaking out, though I don't know why I think that. I mean, he never freaked out when he found out he was going to have to move into his sister's house and raise her children. He didn't freak out when there was projectile vomiting for three days. He didn't freak out when Ashley locked herself in the bathroom with an open bag of flour.

I can almost feel my blood pressure rising, which can't be good for the peanut inside me right now. I guess I'm the one that's freaking out. Not him.

"How can you be so calm? I'm pregnant! A year ago, you didn't even want kids and now you have two ...and a half. You...you...you knocked up your teenaged babysitter. It's like life just keeps taking your choices away from you. Why aren't you mad?"

"As I recall, I really enjoyed knocking up my teenaged babysitter. And the twins are amazing. And I'm in love with you. What's one more kid?"

"Are you serious?"

"Yes."

I force myself to take a calming breath.

"You're not mad or frustrated?"

"No."

And another.

"You don't want me to...make another choice or give it up for adoption?"

Conner slides to the floor in front of my chair and takes my hand. "No. I'll stand by you if that's what you want. But that's not what I want." He brings my bandaged knuckles to his mouth and kisses me softly. "I want you to come home. Come back to me and the girls. They miss you so much. I miss you. It's killing me not being able to take care of you. Not to hold you at night. I almost lost so much the other day. That gunman almost took my life away from me."

My heart is beating so hard. "I miss you guys, too."

"We can do this together, you know. There's not a damn thing *you* can't do, I've seen that firsthand. So together, I figure we're unstoppable."

He really loves me. I don't know how or why I doubted it. "Well, I did take down a would-be carjacker. I suppose I can manage three kids and a bricklayer."

He lays his head on my lap, and I sift my fingers through his hair. "It's gonna be a helluva ride, you know."

Three kids under the age of two. Yeah. It's gonna be crazy.

"People are going to say things, Conner. I imagine my mom has some things to say, too."

"We'll handle it. We're a family, Cassidy." We hear my mom poking around in the kitchen, so he lifts his head. "The girls are going to love having a baby brother or sister."

I sniffle, pretty sure pregnancy hormones are the reason I'm crying. Yeah, for sure. Pregnancy hormones. "Wait. Who is with the girls right now?"

"The three idiots from poker night have been helping out. And Deacon's mom. And your mom."

"My mom?"

"Yeah, she came over for a few hours this morning while I was at work to give Deacon's mom a break."

"She didn't say anything to me."

"She's a good woman. That's where you get it from."

I smile because he's right. But she is still going to chew me a new one.

I ask him to help me pack. I only have a few things left here, anyway. He is getting a kick out of my childhood room.

"It looks like a guest room. Did you never have any rock star posters or anything?"

"I had a Myspace full of emo bands and pink glitter fonts, but my bedroom I've always liked kind of plain."

"Myspace. I forgot about Myspace. You ready?"

I take a good look around. "Take me home, Conner."

Epilogue

Conner

Two years later

The house is a disaster.

As usual.

But my girls are in the bath with their momma, and my son is asleep in my arms in the rocking chair, and despite the fact that I only got to eat two bites of my German chocolate cake tonight before a meltdown from *Hayden* of all people, I'm in a pretty damn good mood.

I put the baby down and search out the girls. They're all three playing tea party in the tub, but it's bedtime for two of them, so Cassidy and I work as a team getting them into dry jammies and into bed. My wife promised me a birthday blowjob tonight, and I am ready to collect, so I take a quick shower, too.

Of course, she's passed out when I come back to the bedroom. Who wouldn't be? Our life is always exhausting. I sigh and tell my dick maybe tomorrow.

As I'm crawling into bed, trying not to wake her, she throws the covers back to reveal some very naughty lingerie.

My dick is instantly hard.

She's gotten curvier since having a baby, and I fucking love it. Every inch of her is lush, begging to be squeezed. I reach for her, but she shakes her head.

"I know what happens if I let you touch me, and it ends with me not getting to suck you off."

"Well, what'd you wear that for then?"

She smiles and straddles me on the bed. "Torture."

The tiny black panties she's wearing are damp. She's ripe and ready, and as much as I want that blowjob, maybe her riding my cock would be better. I get a finger into her panties, but she moves away. Pulling me so that I'm sitting on the edge of the bed with my legs spread wide and she's on her knees in front of me.

Not gonna lie. Part of me is wanting to take her. Just flip her over and claim what's mine right there on the carpet next to our bed. She likes it when I get a little rough with her. And it's my birthday, right?

But she's got her hand wrapped around my cock now, and it'd be a shame to stop her. Cassidy cups my balls in one hand and grasps my shaft with her other. I'm already in heaven. Her long, slow strokes are indeed torturous. The best kind of torture. She adds a twist at the head of my cock, and my body suddenly seizes like I've been shocked.

That's when she adds her tongue, lightly licking me from top to bottom. I groan loudly. It feels so good. Everything feels so good with her. She starts massaging the underside of my cock with that talented tongue, and I am ready to do anything—beg, borrow, steal—if she'd take me all the way in her mouth. But she's a tease, and her favorite thing to do is drive me crazy. So, she takes her time.

"Sweetness, you're killing me."

She just smiles sweetly and goes back to her labor of love on my dick. I'm so hard I could hammer nails, but she's just licking and wetting me up and down. When she finally, finally, takes my cockhead in her mouth, she just holds it there. My chest is heaving, my hands grasping the sheets, and my wife is just holding her lips in a perfect ring around me, waiting for me to lose control. My cock is pulsing angrily, wanting more friction, more heat. Just more. I'm desperate for her.

"Woman, suck me."

Nothing.

"Sweetness, I need you so much. Please."

And then I'm sliding in her mouth. She bobs her head, taking me further every pass. I can't look at her. If I see her pretty mouth wrapped around me, I'll come, and I know she's not done. My fingers dig into her hair, but I resist, barely, the urge to control her head.

I'm feeling it in the base of my spine. It's coming soon. My balls are drawing up. Shit. I'm not going to last. And then slowly, oh so slowly, she takes me in, all the way, inch by fucking inch until I feel the back of her throat. She's swallowing me and that's it. I can't even tell her I'm going to come. My mind is too foggy to form the words. The world tilts, and I'm shooting in her mouth and down her throat. I open my eyes and God bless her, she's swallowing every drop I give her, watching my face while she does it.

That's the hottest thing ever. The eye contact. She absolutely owns my soul. I hold her face gently in my hands while my orgasm tapers off. She plops me out of her mouth and grins. "Happy birthday, Mr. Webster."

"I need five minutes to recover, and then I'm coming for that pussy."

"Five minutes?" She looks dubious. She's not wrong. Even when I was ten years younger, I needed more than five minutes between rounds.

"I'm going to eat you for hours. That will give me plenty of time to recover."

She grins. And then the baby monitor picks up a not so faint cry.

"I'll get him," I say.

No big deal. So, I'll eat her for hours tomorrow night, I think to myself as I change the baby and bring him to bed. One of the perks of being married is that I can make another play again the next night. Or maybe the next morning, depending on how this goes. I can stick this married dick in my wife as often as we want to. No more waiting for the weekend to hook up with strangers. No more awkward "it's been nice, but I gotta go," when I'm done.

I don't even know that guy anymore. This guy, he gets laid a hell of a lot more, but that isn't even the best part. This guy gets to roll over and smell his woman's hair. He gets to look her in the eye and feel something.

He gets to go to sleep knowing he's somebody's whole world and wake up knowing his whole world is right there.

The baby is still getting weaned, so he latches on to his mama for a feeding, and I crawl into bed next to them. She's so beautiful. She's got this glow that attached to her when she was pregnant and just never left. At least not when I'm looking at her.

I'm the luckiest SOB on the planet. If every man loved his wife as much as I love mine, this world would run a whole lot better. Because when you love someone like that, you work real hard being worthy of it. And if everyone just concentrated on being worthy of the person they loved, we'd have a lot fewer problems.

But I can't fix the rest of the world. It's enough trying to keep this crazy ship afloat. Three kids, man. Nothing about it is easy. But it's worth every sleepless night and every dirty diaper and every frayed nerve.

I'll never be the intellectual in a room. I'll never be a billionaire or a rock star or a professional ball player. I don't sparkle in the sun or turn into a wolf when things get dicey. But to my wife and my three kids, I'm a hero.

And that's all that really matters.

WELL, READER, I HOPE you enjoyed that as much as I enjoyed writing it. Cassidy and Conner were so very dirty—yet ohmygosh—wasn't he the most lovable hero ever? I mean, c'mon. Conner was all tough guy on the outside, but he had the biggest, sweetest heart ever.

Well, except maybe for the hero of my *next* book who is retiring from the Army and doesn't feel like he deserves to be loved. Luckily, I paired him up with Emily who...well, okay, she doesn't feel like she deserves to be loved, either. But you know I only write happy endings, so I'm sure it will work out. Keep reading for a sneak peek of *Tagged*. My first Christmas book in the Blue Collar Bad Boys series.

Cheers,
Brill

IF YOU'RE TIRED OF billionaires, maybe you're ready for some real men. Dirty, hardworking, and good with their hands are the kind of heroes you'll find in the *Blue Collar Bad Boy Series*. These guys aren't cultured. They are hot *AF* alpha heroes who know how to take care of the slightly nerdy women they fall for. For reals, this series is more fun than you knew you were missing. And they don't need to be read in order.

So which blue collar bad boy will you choose next? They are all rough, raw, and surprisingly sweet.

Like...the roadhouse bouncer and the actuarial sciences student in *Bounced*[1].

Or...the carpenter and the Jeopardy! nerd in *Nailed*[2].

Perhaps...the oil rigger and the kindergarten teacher in *Drilled*[3].

Mayhap...the tow truck driver and the sorority uptown girl in *Wrecked*[4].

---

1.   *https://books2read.com/Bounced*

2.   *https://books2read.com/Nailed*

3.   *https://books2read.com/Drilled*

4.   *https://books2read.com/wrecked*

Surely...the brick layer hot single dad and the babysitter in *Laid*[5].

How about...a returning military hero and the wallflower at Christmas in *Tagged*[6]?

Or...the farmer who needs a wife and wants the curvy waitress in *Plowed*[7]?

Or...the hot rancher trying to convince the city girl to stay in *Bucked*[8]?

Maybe...the bomb squad cop and his pregnant neighbor? Did I mention she's a virgin? You read that right. Try *Banged*[9].

And surely...the modern day Viking bartender and the bookworm virgin in *Tapped*[10]?

About the author

LIKE FIRST TIMES? FORBIDDEN fruit? *Yes, please.*

Love a hot, dominant alpha claiming what's his? *Fuck, yeah.*

Want to watch him fall hard for the sweetest fantasy he didn't know he needed? Me too!

---

5.   *https://books2read.com/laid*

6.   *https://books2read.com/tagged*

7.   *https://books2read.com/plowed*

8.   *https://books2read.com/bucked*

9.   *https://books2read.com/banged*

10.   *https://books2read.com/Tapped-A-Blue-Collar-Bad-Boy-Book*

I'm Brill Harper and I love happily ever afters, smokin' hot bad boys, and quirky, often nerdy, heroines that I'd love to be friends with off page. These ladies are not perfect—but they're perfect for one man—and he's always sexy AF.

Seriously—these heroes only have one weakness, and it's sticky, sweet love. They don't let anything stand in the way of taking what belongs to them. When it comes to the women they love, it's hard cocks, dirty talk, and soft, mushy heart feels.

*Brill is a sooper sekrit penname for a better known author who just can't handle all the dirty. She can't handle it...but can you?

BookBub[11]

---

11.   https://www.bookbub.com/authors/brill-harper